Penny Hen

Barbara deRubertis
Illustrated by Eva Vagreti Cockrille

The Kane Press
New York

Cover Design: Sheryl Kagen

Library of Congress Catalog Card Number: 96-75012

ISBN 1-57565-001-0

10 9 8 7 6 5 4 3

First published in the United States of America in 1997 by The Kane Press.
Printed in Mexico

LET'S READ TOGETHER is a registered trademark of The Kane Press.

Jenny has
a new pet hen.
Her name is Penny—
Penny Hen.

3

Jenny sets her
Penny Hen
in the hen house
in the pen.

4

Penny Hen can
fix her nest.
Jenny helps her
fix the rest.

Jenny says, "If all goes well, I will soon have eggs to sell.

"Then I'll get two more pet hens. I saw them in the pet shop pens.

"I will name one new hen Bess. And I will name the other Tess."

Jenny fixes
two more nests.
Penny Hen just
sits and rests.

9

"I don't want to
share my pen
with Bess or Tess
or ANY hen!

"I'm the very
best pet hen.
I want to be the
ONLY hen!

"I will bend and
stretch my neck.

"Then I'll peck and
peck and peck.

12

"I'll make the nests
a messy mess.

"A mess for Bess!

"A mess for Tess!

14

"And there will be no eggs for Jenny. She will NOT get eggs from Penny!"

Jenny steps
into the pen.
What a mess!
What a hen!

Jenny stops.
She will not yell
at Penny Hen
for she can tell...

that Penny Hen
is most upset.
So Jenny helps
her little pet.

"Penny, I will
fix your nest.
I'll fix the mess.
And you can rest.

"There will be
no nest for Bess.
There will be
no nest for Tess.

"You can be my *only* pet.
You can be my *lonely* pet!"

A *lonely* pet?
Penny frets.
Should she welcome
two new pets?

Look at Penny
fix this nest!
A nest for Bess!
She does her best.

Look at Penny
fix that nest!
A nest for Tess!
Soon she can rest.

Then she lays
an egg for Jenny.
This egg is a
gift from Penny.

This egg has
a pretty shell.
This is one that
she can sell.

Jenny sees
the nest for Bess!
Jenny sees
the nest for Tess!

Then she sees
the egg for Jenny.
What a pretty
gift from Penny!

"Thank you, thank you,
Penny Hen!
Thank you, thank you,
Penny Friend!"

Now Bess and Tess
are in the pen
with their new friend—
Penny Hen!